*What do you call a
bee born in May?*

A maybee!

Spelling Bee

Queen Elizabee

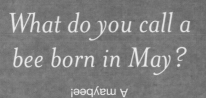

a-p-i-p-h-o-b-i-a

Why do bees buzz?

Because they can't whistle!

*What do bees do if they want to
use public transportation?*

Wait at a buzz stop!

Buzzz Lightyear

*What is a bee's favorite
classical music composer?*

Bee-thoven!

Wanna Bee

*Who writes books
for little bees?*

Bee-trix Potter!

Aunt Bee

Miss Beehave

Can bees fly in the rain?

Not without their little yellow jackets!

All profits from the sale of this book will be allocated

to those affected with Multiple Sclerosis with the hope that

within our lifetime MS will stand for "Mystery Solved".

Acknowledgements

Kristin Blackwood

Mike Blanc

Sheila Tarr

Robin Hegan

Trio Design & Marketing Communications Inc.
Jennie Levy Smith, David Buehler

Kurt Landefeld

Dave Shoenfelt

Dennis Roliff

Joseph D. Varley, M.D.
Chairman, Department of Psychiatry, Summa Health System

Dr. Ivonne H. Hobfoll
Clinical Psychologist, Summa Health System

Dr. Janet Stadulis

Paul Royer

Kathryn DeLong

Julianne Stein

Let Me Bee
VanitaBooks, LLC
All rights reserved.
© 2008 VanitaBooks, LLC

Text by Vanita Oelschlager.
Illustrations by Kristin Blackwood.
Title lettering and bio illustrations by Mike Blanc.
Designed by Trio Design & Marketing Communications Inc.
Photo by Dave Shoenfelt.
Printed in China.
ISBN 978-0-9800162-1-5

www.VanitaBooks.com

Let Me Bee

Vanita Oelschlager

illustrated by

Kristin Blackwood

This book is dedicated to

Cheyanne

Andrew

and

my other grandchildren.

Merciful heavens!
And fiddle-dee-dee!
Why would a kid
Be afraid of a bee?

If only you knew
How big YOU seem to me.
I'm a dot in the sky
You're the size of a tree!

If I'm on a flower
And look at your knee,
It's bigger than anything
Else I can see.

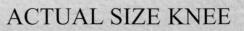

ACTUAL SIZE KNEE

Ms. Bee, you don't get it.
You look huge to me.
Go fly somewhere else.
Up a hill – out to sea!

You don't know how I feel
When I see a bee –
And it seems like they always
Come straight after me!

Bees of all sizes
Just hide in their hive,
Watching and waiting
For me to arrive.

Bees look for kids.
That's what they do.
Bees want their stingers
To get stuck in you!

I'm no wasp or a hornet,
I'm a sweet honeybee.
I don't think you're seeing
The actual me.

If I thought my life
Were in danger, you see,
My stinging you
Would surely end ME!

No, I've got my work.
It's what bees do best.
Taking pollen to plants
And nectar to our nest.

Flying flower to flower
And back to the hive,
We're making the honey
That keeps us alive.

We buzz 'cause we're happy
In all that we do,
It's like purring, for cats...
Or singing, for you.

Well, when I go outside,
I look really hard,
To make sure I don't see you
Buzzing my yard.

You're always around.
I know what I see.
I bet you're just waiting
For a chance to sting me!

Mom says bees are good
And we need them on earth.
I think you sting kids
That's your mission from birth.

If you look very closely
And watch what I do,
You'll see that I'm not at all
Focused on you.

I carry pollen
From flower to flower
And help farmers grow crops
Every day...every hour.
The bee is not counted
As one of life's shirkers –
We're some of this planet's
Very best workers.

My family and I live
In a group called a colony.
We have workers and drones
And our beloved queen bee.

We call our babies larvae
And team with each other
To care for our young ones
And our precious queen mother.

We're really as sweet
As the honey we make.
Thinking we want to hurt you
Is just a mistake.

But I can't have a picnic
In the grass or by a tree.
Bees love sandwiches,
Sodas, suckers – and me!

You want me to like you?
But you're mean, ugly, and fat.
How do you think
You can help me with that?

I once asked my mother
What jobs I could do
With no bees around
Not even a few.
USS BEELESS
She said, on the ocean
A big sailing boat
Wouldn't have any bees,
'Cause they can't stay afloat!

And the North Pole, she said.
It might be bee-free.
But there aren't many jobs
And no people to see.
I could be an astronaut
And fly into space.
No bees out there,
Not even a trace!

Apiphobia

Now stop it, you two.
I have heard quite enough!
We all need each other,
So don't talk so tough.

The word "Apiphobia"
Stands for this fear
That lots of kids have
When a bee gets too near.

There are so many things
That you can do
To make sure apiphobia
Never happens to you.

Read books about bees
And articles, too.
Go to insect exhibits
Down at the zoo.

I can catch you a bee
In a big glass jar.
Then we'll let it go free
To fly home or fly far.

If you get really scared,
You can just go inside.
While it isn't much fun,
It's a safe place to hide.

At picnics, you could wrap
Yourself up, I suppose.
But you won't be too comfy
Inside all those clothes.

Remember, bees help us
Grow flowers and fruits,
Without them, we're left with
Just stems, seeds, and roots.

We can both feel safe.
I'll be hived with the bees,
And you'll live with your family,
Wherever you please.

The next time you see me
On your porch or back shed,
Don't swat me or chase me.
Just watch me instead.

We can sit side by side,
Watch the world going by.
And we'll count all our blessings,
And be friends, you and I.

Remember the lesson
We've learned, making friends.
We learned it together:
Life starts where fear ends.

Illustration Technique

I enjoy using different techniques and materials when creating
a work of art. The illustrations in *Let Me Bee* are no exception.
These illustrations are made from rough-textured watercolor paper.
They come to life with gouache paint and pen. Each piece is cut out by
hand from the paper, arranged at different heights and angles to create
shadows, and then photographed. The inspiration for my paintings
comes from the wonderful and playful spirit of my mother, the author.
I hope that both children and adults will enjoy this adorable book.

A special thanks goes to Mike Blanc.
His creative and technical guidance have been
a blessing on this project. For me,
my best work comes through the
collaboration of our wonderful team.

~ Kristin Blackwood ~

Vanita Oelschlager

I write books about things that happen in my life. This book was inspired by one of my grandchildren, who had a fear of bees. His fear was real. Like many fears, it was irrational (he wasn't allergic to stings). It was also incapacitating. I wanted to help him and other children (and adults too!) understand where fear comes from and how to deal with it — and to understand that leading a fearless life can open onto a world full of joy and endless possibility.

Kristin Blackwood

When I was a little girl I had a huge fear of bees — actually anything that bizz-buzzed around. I am happy to report that I have learned to embrace and love bees for their wonderful contribution to our planet. I hope to carry on the bee-loving tradition with my two young daughters. During the production of this book, I conquered my fear of dimensional drawing by using the cut-and-stack paper technique. It was fun to experiment with this form of art and to work closely with Vanita, the author, who is also my mother.

fear-free

Vanita and her grandchildren.

What goes zzub, zzub?

A bee flying backwards!

Glory Bee

Fumble Bee

What do you get if you cross
a bee with a skunk?

An animal that stinks and stings!

What do you call
a baby bee?

A little humbug!

Wasabee

What did the bee
say to the flower?

Hello, honey!

What do you call a bee that's
had a spell put on him?

He's bee-witched!

Why do bees hum?

Because they forgot the words!

To Bee

or

Not To Bee

What are the
smartest bees called?

Spelling Bees!